Marketing Yourself

SfEP Guides

The SfEP Guides series is intended for copy-editors and proofreaders, both practising and potential, and other people involved in publishing, whether in the formal or informal sectors. The authors are usually senior members of the SfEP, and publications in the series focus on the core disciplines of copy-editing and proofreading, while also extending occasionally into related fields such as project management and web editing.

Other Guides in the series are:

Editing Fiction: A short introduction, by Imogen Olsen

Editing into Plain Language: Working for non-publishers, by Sarah Carr

Editor and Client: Building a professional relationship, by Anne Waddingham

Pricing a Project: How to prepare a professional quotation, by Melanie Thompson

Starting Out: Setting up a small business, 3rd edition, by Valerie Rice

Theses and Dissertations: Checking the language, by Pat Baxter

Your House Style: Styling your words for maximum impact, by Christina Thomas

Marketing Yourself

Strategies to promote your editorial business

second edition

Sara Hulse

society for editors
and proofreaders

s*f*ep

Marketing Yourself

Strategies to promote your editorial business

2nd edition

Sara Hulse

society for editors
and proofreaders   s*f*ep

First published as *Developing a Marketing Strategy* in 2008
This edition published 2013

Published by the Society for Editors and Proofreaders
Apsley House
176 Upper Richmond Road
London SW15 2SH

sfep.org.uk

ISBN 978-0-9563164-7-9

The information contained in this work is accurate and current to the best of the author's knowledge. The author and publisher, however, make no guarantee as to, and assume no responsibility for, the correctness, sufficiency or completeness of such information or recommendation.

Editor: Gillian Clarke

Designed by Helius

Typeset by M Rules

Printed in the UK by The Printing House, London

Contents

Acknowledgements   vi

1   Why do you need a marketing plan or strategy?   1

2   Getting started   2
    Take an honest look at your business and define your skills   2
    Promote yourself: getting the word out   2
    Identifying and targeting clients   4

3   Which marketing methods are right for you?   5
    Your website   6
    Directories and advertising   6
    Cold contact: letters, emails and phone calls   8
    Networking   9
        Face-to-face networking   9
        Social media   11
        Building relationships with your clients   11

4   Putting your plan together   13

5   Implementing your plan and measuring its effectiveness   15

Appendix   16
    A basic checklist   16
    Resources   17
    Websites   18
    Business support and networking organisations   18

Acknowledgements

I am indebted to the many freelance colleagues I have met and chatted to over the years for their examples of good practice, and to the many clients I have worked with for giving me much valuable experience. Together they have provided me with much of the material in this booklet.

I also thank Penny Poole and Krysia Johnson for providing valuable feedback on early versions of the Guide.

Opinions expressed are my own, and are not officially those of the SfEP. I apologise in advance for any errors or omissions and hope that, if there are any, they do not detract from the information provided.

Sara Hulse
August 2013

1 Why do you need a marketing plan or strategy?

As an editorial freelance you may think that marketing isn't relevant to you, but it's vital to think of yourself as a business owner who is offering a service, or range of services. You need to have a marketing plan or strategy and to be proactive to sell what you do and to generate leads. Increasing competition means that many of us are having to expand our areas of expertise and seek new clients. Others who are just starting out may have no idea how to target markets or find clients that fit with their skill set. This Guide is designed to give your 'marketing department' a jump start!

In simple terms, your potential clients need to know who you are and what you do, and your existing clients need to know about all the services you offer and the sort of projects you've worked on. The aim of developing a marketing plan is to map out how to do this: which steps and techniques are right for you, and how and when you're going to use them. You should detail whom you intend to target, and how you'll let them know about your services – hopefully without spending a fortune. After all, you may be the best editor or proofreader in the world, but, if nobody knows you exist, you're going to struggle to make a living.

You may be perfectly happy with the amount of work you have and with your current clients, and so don't need to market yourself. But don't forget that every year, through no fault of your own, you'll lose a number of your clients through relocation, competition, change of business, closure or contacts moving on. So, even to stay still, you need to have some way of replacing these clients. You need to protect yourself from future changes in the market – for example, a publisher taking all of their proofreading work in-house, or sending it overseas. Many of us are guilty of relying on a small number of clients, and on 'word of mouth' to gain new clients, and, if we do any marketing at all, it tends to be reactive and sporadic.

As you go through the process of creating a marketing plan for your business, keep in mind that marketing is not a one-off activity, but rather an ongoing process. Your marketing efforts should focus on getting plenty of new clients coming in, lots of inactive clients coming back and all your current clients using you more.

2 Getting started

Take an honest look at your business and define your skills

The first step is to review your current situation – you need to define your business as it stands now and assess your personal strengths, skills and resources. What services do you offer? Be very clear about this and about what you can and can't do. What are your areas of expertise? Could you learn new skills in order to offer a wider range of services? When companies are looking for freelance support, it's usually because they need someone with specific knowledge that isn't available within their business. So it's better to be a specialist than to say 'I can work on any subject'.

We're all competing against many others offering very similar services, so think about what makes you unique. At the very least, try to differentiate yourself in some way from the competition – are you able to turn work around quickly, or work in-house, or do you offer project management, for instance?

> **Tip**
> - Gather all your CVs, samples of work, etc, together when you make a start – you'll be amazed at the wealth of experience you have, but it's really useful to have it all in one place. Think about *all* the skills you can offer potential clients.

Promote yourself: getting the word out

Editorial freelances are no different from other small businesses, even if you work alone and operate as a sole trader. You still need to develop a professional business image. A distinctive company name, business cards and letterheads will all help, and initial costs don't have to be high.

You also need to develop a clear, concise and memorable message that communicates what it is you do. It's important to focus on the benefits of what you do – your message should answer the client's question 'What's in it for me?' and not leave them asking 'So what?' You may need slightly different versions, depending on whether you're talking to a publisher or a potential client outside the publishing world. To some people, being an editor means working on a newspaper or magazine, and they may have no concept of what a copy-editor or proofreader is, or that's there any difference between them!

Make sure you promote all of your skills. Someone may appreciate your marketing, administrative, teaching or IT skills as well as your proofreading and editing ones, especially in the non-publishing sector. Be confident – bring what you know to the table and don't be shy about selling it.

Tip
- Test out your marketing message on friends and family – do they understand what you're trying to say? You should be able to get across to someone what you do in just a sentence, so think carefully about your choice of words and how to deliver them with the most impact.

To begin with, you might simply want to produce a short CV and an A4 sheet describing your services. But whatever format you choose, make sure it looks professional – and doesn't contain a single error! You can develop a 'basic' version that you can update every month or so with information about recent projects and new clients – and perhaps different versions for different types of client (publisher/non-publisher). Work towards building up a portfolio of your work, so that potential clients can see what sorts of projects you've worked on. You may like to include pictures of books/journals/magazines you've worked on (making sure you get the client's permission before you do this), but keep your messages straightforward and simple. You have only a few seconds at most to engage your reader and persuade them to read the rest of the copy. Therefore, it's vital that your message stands out and makes it clear what you are offering.

Many clients, especially publishers, will still ask for a CV, but a standard chronological CV – showing an unbroken employment history of positions with steadily increasing responsibility designed to get you to the next rung of the corporate ladder – is useless for the freelance. You need to develop a functional, or skills-based, CV that gives details of your skills, abilities and accomplishments, and that can be 'tweaked' depending on who will be receiving it. Clients needing editorial assistance are looking to offer work to someone skilled and reliable – your functional CV will highlight your skills; your list of clients will reassure them that you can do the work on offer.

You may want to develop a strap-line slogan for your business, and perhaps a logo. Use this on business cards, your stationery, website, etc, to create and communicate your brand. Think long and hard about your logo. It speaks volumes about your business and will hopefully be widely distributed, so it's important to get it right.

Your business cards should state clearly who you are and give a good indication of what you do – because people will forget. If someone picks up your business card again a year after they've met you, it's no good simply having your name on it, or even the name of your business if it doesn't convey exactly what you do. Plus, of course, it needs to have your full (and up-to-date) contact details, and your website address. Always carry your business cards with you and hand them out at every opportunity. It's amazing where they end up and they can sometimes produce work from the unlikeliest of sources. They're a very cheap way to get information about yourself and your business out to the wider world.

The important thing is to make sure that all your marketing materials – stationery, business cards, brochures, website – have consistent branding; use the same typeface(s), and don't tinker with your logo. Use the same photos across your website, LinkedIn, Twitter, etc. If you're not happy to use a personal photo, you could use all or part of your logo. Remember that for things such as Twitter only a small image can be displayed, so it's really useful to have a logo that you can use just a part of for things like this.

Identifying and targeting clients

You need to think about whether you want to be making more money, working for a wider range of clients or doing more interesting work – or would you like more regular work/projects? It's worth trying to describe the attributes of your ideal client and preferred work. For example: is this client someone who pays on time, offers good rates, is located nearby (so you can go into the office for meetings, etc), appreciates quality/what you do, is loyal and repeatedly comes back to you with new projects, or is simply someone 'nice' to work with?

Tip
- Write out in paragraph form a description of your ideal client or the type of client you are trying to attract. If you don't know whom you're trying to attract, you're not going to know how to go about it. Taking the time to really think about your potential clients is a very useful step.

You may need to develop different approaches for different types of client – or publishers as opposed to non-publishers, for example, or for students and academics as opposed to commercial clients.

Think about the particular challenges that each client faces and how you can help meet them. Every client will have different needs, depending on the organisation and the project in hand. One might need people who can turn work around at short notice. Another might be seeking freelances who specialise in a given field, and so need editors who can really engage with the subject matter, or who can liaise effectively with authors.

Clients like to work with freelances who inspire confidence. As a freelance, it's easy to feel like a very passive party, waiting humbly for the all-powerful client to give you some work. But for a client, the most appealing freelances are those who are confident in their skills and are able to empathise with their needs.

3 Which marketing methods are right for you?

This step needs some brainstorming and research. But if you're clear about your capabilities and what you're trying to achieve, the decision about how to promote yourself and your business effectively becomes a matter of common sense.

Take a look around – use your existing connections with other freelances to find out what they're doing to market their businesses that's working for them. Obviously you don't want to copy anything that someone else is doing, but you can certainly create a version that fits your business. You can follow other editors on social media outlets such as Twitter, LinkedIn and Facebook. Become their fans, become an active member in their online groups, and really get to know their businesses. See how they share information on these networks, the type of information they share, and when they share it. You can learn a lot from your fellow editorial professionals.

It's important to remember that some methods will work better for you than others, and even that different approaches work at different stages of a business. In your early days, advertising on directory websites might give you a good start, but later on you may find that most of your jobs come from clients you've already worked for.

Your website

There's no doubt that a website is a vital marketing tool – it lends professional authority, makes you easy to find, shows that you use current technology, and lets you tell a more in-depth and up-to-date story about your business than a CV or leaflet can. You can include information about recent projects, your skills and qualifications, the nature of the work you're seeking, and your business terms and conditions.

It may not be the best way of attracting new clients but is a great way of providing further information to potential clients who have found you by other means. Include your web address in your email signature and on all your business stationery.

Of course, creating and maintaining a professional-looking website takes time – it will need constant updating and review – and can be costly in terms of set-up and ongoing development costs. But perhaps you could 'trade' skills – if you know a website designer, perhaps they could design you a website at a discounted rate in exchange for you proofreading website content for their clients.

> **Tips**
> - Get yourself a professional email address (ie not Yahoo, AOL or Hotmail), a domain name and a simple website. It doesn't need to win any prizes for design or slick copy, but it does need to look professional.
> - Writing copy for the web is a particular skill, and if you don't have experience in this area it's worth spending part of your budget on having it done professionally. If you do opt to do it yourself, make sure you get some sort of objective external review of your work. Look at the websites of other freelances to get inspiration (but obviously don't copy their ideas!).

Directories and advertising

Many publishers say that the SfEP directory is the first place they look for freelances, so it has to be worthwhile upgrading your membership to Ordinary/Advanced, if you haven't done so already. If you're still an Associate, don't forget that you can be listed in Associates Available, another valuable means of getting work.

Some SfEP local groups publish their own 'mini-directories', or act as an informal means of passing on excess work or recommending other members for work one of the group isn't able to do.

Organisations you can join, such as the Federation of Small Businesses or British Chambers of Commerce, publish directories of members. Other specialist organisations with their own directories (eg the National Union of Journalists, Chartered Institute of Marketing) may be worth looking into.

And then of course there are various specialist directory sites (the details of some of which are listed in the Appendix), which offer the option of being able to target anyone who is directly looking for your products or services. The advantages of these are that the work on offer can be very varied, and often pays better than work being offered by traditional publishers. The downside is that you're advertising alongside a lot of other people; often the client's deadline is extremely tight; there may be a fee involved; and the time taken to respond to enquiries may achieve nothing. But there's always going to be an element of that, however you advertise.

Some people seem to get a steady stream of work from key directories and listings, but few seem to rely on them as a primary marketing tool. Competition is high, so make your directory or listing entry stand out. Be clever about what you say about yourself – use key words to highlight your skills rather than lengthy text. Look at existing listings to see what's effective and eye-catching. You should mention the areas in which you have experience and expertise, but many people have picked up leads from more niche areas such as cookery or archaeology. Avoid saying that you can work on anything – potential clients might infer that you are a jack of all trades but master of none.

Tip
- Prepare a list of questions for a potential new client and keep it by the phone – you never know when someone might call in response to a directory entry.

Advertising is generally an expensive option, but agencies that specialise in working with small businesses can be found in directories such as *Yellow Pages* and are often more flexible, as well as being cheaper, than larger agencies. Some publications may help you create the advert you place with them. Simply supply them with a logo and the wording you've drafted and they'll often design it for you at no extra cost.

Of course, advertising doesn't have to cost a lot. In some cases it can be free, such as listings in free local business directories, *Yellow Pages*, TouchLocal, etc. It's a good idea to register with as many of these as you can. The downside is that you might receive lots of calls trying to sell you products and services.

Cold contact: letters, emails and phone calls

Avoid sending an 'academic' CV if it's full of interesting but almost completely irrelevant experience – concentrate on developing a 'functional' CV or profile instead (see page 3). The main thing is to keep it short and relevant – and updated!

Develop a covering letter that you can send by post or email and adapt it as appropriate for different potential clients. Focus on how your knowledge/ training/experience matches their requirements. And make sure your email or letter doesn't contain a single mistake! It's important to identify beforehand the name of the person in a company who allocates work to freelances. This isn't always easy, and might entail making a couple of phone calls to the company first, but it's worth putting in the effort beforehand to find the right person.

Consider your timing: mail your CV before busy periods – such as just before Christmas or the summer holidays – but don't send it when people aren't likely to be in the office. And it's really important to follow up what you've sent. Even if someone says they don't need anyone just now but might do so in the future, make contact again every three or six months and give them an update of what you've done that might make you more credible than last time.

Tip
- If someone approaches you about work, even if you can't take on the job, ask if you can send them your up-to-date profile/CV for future reference – that way the client is more likely to come back to you for future projects. This can be a very effective strategy, particularly with publishers.

Cold calling is probably the least favourite marketing method among freelances! If you can do it, cold calling can bring rewards, but you should be prepared for a lot of point-blank refusals, people who don't really know what you're talking about, and having to make repeated calls to reach the person you want. However, it can be very worthwhile, with one 'hit' making up for many more 'misses'.

As with sending out a CV or an email, there's a strong element of luck – you may just happen to call when someone has a job sitting on their desk waiting to be sent out. You have to be able to sell yourself, and to sound professional, competent, confident and reliable. Don't put people on the spot, but make sure they know you're interested in working for them.

> **Tips**
> - Have a prepared script written down before your call.
> - Always check with the person that it's a good time for them to talk; arrange to call back if necessary.
> - Approach people in a business-like way, but be friendly and polite, too. People want to think they can work with you.
> - Keep track of whom you've called and the responses, and follow up positive replies quickly by sending further information.

Try to find out the name of the person you need to speak to in advance, as switchboards are often briefed to ward off salespeople, which in this case means you! Saying 'Can I speak to someone who commissions freelances someone in the editorial department?' is a sure sign that you don't have an existing relationship with the organisation and is likely to yield only a brick wall. You may find the information on the company website, or you might need to call them to try to get a name – you can then call again to try to speak to that person. If you do manage to have a brief conversation with someone, follow it up by referring them to your website or sending further information. You'll probably then need to follow up with another call to refresh their memory.

Networking

Face-to-face networking

Opportunities for networking include everything from SfEP local groups to events organised by business-support organisations. And of course the annual SfEP conference is the best place to meet like-minded people and share your experiences and ideas with others. But simply keeping in touch with current or previous clients is an important form of networking.

Tip

- If you possibly can, join your local SfEP group – people are very generous with their time and experience, and are more likely to pass on work they can't take on themselves if they've met you and you've made a good impression! The friendships developed in local groups can forge strong business links – people share tips and ideas, contact details of potential clients and work opportunities. If there isn't a local group you feel you can travel to, think about setting one up. If you live in an isolated area, consider setting up a virtual group where you can communicate with others in a similar situation by email, conference call or Skype.

If you do opt to try some face-to-face networking, put together a short statement about what you do – you need to be able to speak confidently about the services you offer and how they can benefit a potential client. This is sometimes referred to as your 'elevator pitch', on the basis that you need to be able to explain to someone exactly what it is you do in the time you have with them in a lift. Make sure you take along plenty of business cards with you and hand out as many as you can. But remember that it's a two-way process. You might not get work directly from someone you meet at a networking event, but, if you can put people you meet in touch with one another, they'll remember you at a later date or recommend you to someone else.

Remember to follow up with a call or short email. If you've put in the effort to go to an event, made initial contact with a potential client and perhaps even sent them some information about what you do, it's criminal to miss out on possible work later because you didn't follow up at the opportune time.

Of course this sort of networking can be costly in terms of time – and some organisations charge people to attend their events. It can take years for work to materialise, so it's important not to give up on contacts you make until you're sure nothing is going to come of it.

Remember that you'll be mingling with people from all sorts of businesses, not just within the publishing world, and they won't necessarily know what a copy-editor or proofreader is – or even that there's a difference. Listen to what business people are asking for, as they might not use the same kind of editorial language. If they talk about needing a 'human spell-check' or a 'sanity check', don't respond with lengthy discussion of BSI symbols and widows and orphans.

Social media

Perhaps rather than 'social media', a better description of Twitter, LinkedIn and Facebook might be 'online business media networks'. You need to think carefully how you're going to utilise these networks and how much time you're going to allocate to them. Reports from editorial freelancers vary as to how much direct work they generate, but some people seem to find them useful for 'passive marketing' – in other words simply having a presence on them and being fairly visible without using them to directly sell their services.

Using them effectively is all about sharing – being prepared to promote the work, skills and resources of others as well as promoting yourself. All of them allow you to showcase your skills and experience, and to some extent you can design your space in a way that is specific to your business and branding. LinkedIn is probably the most useful to editorial freelances, and is becoming an increasingly important search tool for those looking for providers of editorial services. Facebook is perhaps the least useful and most people seem to advocate having a Facebook profile for personal use and a Facebook page for your business.

Tip
- Make sure that, whichever of these networks you use, your details are consistent throughout – and with other promotional items such as your business stationery, website, SfEP directory entry, CV/profile, etc.

There's no financial outlay involved – the only costs are in your time – so it makes sense to take advantage of the excellent networking opportunities these platforms provide. They may not directly provide a source of work, but you may well get found by a potential client, and it all helps to get your name 'out there'.

Building relationships with your clients

It's also vital to keep in touch with your existing clients, whether you're currently working for them or not. If you're working on a project for them, keep them updated of progress; if you haven't worked for them for a while, pick up the phone occasionally or drop them a quick email to ask if they have any projects coming up that you might be able to help them with. If you're in touch with them regularly, they're more likely to use you, or to recommend you to colleagues. And if/when a hiccup does appear on a particular project, they're more likely to be understanding if you have a good relationship with them. It's a great idea to meet clients personally if you possibly can.

It's important to get the balance right between keeping in regular touch and pestering people. You can do things such as sending them a Christmas email saying how much you look forward to working with them in the New Year. Alert clients to when you're going to be away on holiday, but also let them know when you'll be available to take on more work.

Keeping in touch also means that you're more likely to know if they're about to move elsewhere – in which case you can ask them to take your details to their next position and/or pass your details to whoever is replacing them – this can be a really good way of gaining a new client.

Use a bit of bluffing: never say 'I haven't got anything lined up for weeks'. Instead, if you're emailing a previous contact, say 'I'm just coming to the end of a project and am looking at planning my time for the next few months . . . ' and offer to help them – many are very grateful. Beware sending frequent emails saying 'I'm available', as it implies you're quite frequently stuck for work, which doesn't make a good impression.

When you finish a project, always email your contact at the end to say how much you've enjoyed it and that you'd like to work with them again in the future. If they're impressed with your work they'll be only too pleased not to have to search for someone new for their next project.

Tip
- Don't specifically ask for repeat business – you need to encourage it by doing a good job for a fair price and being flexible and easy to work with. Clients will be really happy to find someone they can trust to deliver what they want, on time and to budget, and whom they feel understands them and the work on offer, with whom they feel comfortable. Building rapport that inspires such trust is important.

Word of mouth works wonders, and referrals and recommendations can be one of the most powerful marketing tools. It's a great way of getting new clients because it involves no cost to you. But you need to be proactive. Whenever anyone says anything positive about your work, ask if they would be willing to provide a testimonial for you. The more testimonials you put together, the more confident your prospective clients will be of the service you're offering. Put them on your website – potential clients can feel quite vulnerable when approaching someone new, so, when they can see positive feedback from people in their exact role in comparable organisations, it helps them feel more confident about using you.

In editorial freelancing generally, it's rare for us to receive comments on our work – unless it's very bad – and we often don't even see the finished product. So it can be difficult to get feedback/endorsements, and you'll almost certainly have to ask for them. But also make sure you act on any feedback you do get, and take every opportunity to ask clients what they think about your work.

4 Putting your plan together

By now you're probably suffering from information overload. There are so many techniques, resources and events you can use to promote your services, it may seem like an overwhelming task to get started. Luckily, you don't have to do it all at once.

Your marketing plan will start with the general and move towards specifics. Whether you're writing your first marketing plan or updating an existing one, start with just an outline of the information your plan should contain. Of course there are formal templates you can use to create your own marketing plan, but, because you're the one who has to implement it, you're better off constructing a plan you understand and can use rather than one that follows a template.

> **Tip**
> * Start small and build on it. If you don't know where to start, or don't feel up to setting yourself specific marketing goals or objectives, just spend some time thinking about who your clients might be and where they might look for your services. Even such vague ideas can evolve and adapt over time into your marketing plan.

Your marketing plan needs to include:

* where you're at now (analysis)
* where you want to get to (objectives)
* how you're planning to get there (strategy).

You can break the objectives and strategy parts down into years (ie this year/next year/the following year) to help with your thinking. When setting your marketing objectives, be specific and include measurable goals and a deadline to make it easier to measure your progress.

The bottom line is that you have to know whom you're trying to attract, what you want to accomplish with your marketing efforts, and how you're going to let potential clients know you exist. Your marketing plan should address how you plan to:

- retain existing clients (particularly your best 20%);
- encourage your existing clients to use you more often/regularly;
- find new clients with the same needs as your existing clients.

It's important not to forget your existing clients when putting together your marketing plan, if only because it costs far less to keep an existing client than to find a new one. An analysis of your client base may well reveal that the Pareto effect, or the 80/20 rule, applies: that 80% of your income is generated by 20% of your clients. This is not a problem as long as you know which clients make up the 20%, so that you can focus your resources and efforts on them.

Talking of resources and efforts raises the question of how much time you should allocate to marketing. Everyone will have their own ideas about this, but the important thing is to treat it as a proper 'job'. An intensive effort can bring results both immediately and in the long term. If you can afford to dedicate an entire day to marketing, go for it. If not, why not start or end your day with an hour of marketing? Or rather than setting aside time explicitly you could, depending on your workload, 'allow' yourself time during the working day to interact on LinkedIn, Twitter, SfEPLine and other forums, either at lunchtime or when you reach a natural break point in whatever you're working on. If you don't take your marketing seriously, make time for it and put effort into it, you won't see any results.

Put simply, the focus of your marketing plan should be on gaining new customers, persuading current customers to buy more often and getting inactive customers to return. It should be short, concise and easy to understand. And just writing it all down on paper makes it more likely that you will achieve your goals.

As your business evolves, your marketing plan should evolve with it. It should become almost second nature to review your plan as new avenues open up to you, or indeed as old ones become less attractive. Think about the future. Always be thinking about where the next project is coming from, as well as more long-term plans about the future of your business.

5 Implementing your plan and measuring its effectiveness

Whilst the planning phase of creating the marketing plan is the key to getting your marketing in motion, implementing it is paramount. If you just let the plan sit and collect dust, you've simply wasted your time, and you're certainly not going to see the results that constant and consistent marketing brings.

You may have been marketing your business for years and continue to do the same things without really taking the time to determine how well your efforts are working out for you. Take a look at what you've been doing to market your business and measure the results of each effort. Decide if there are ways you can mimic the positive results your marketing efforts have brought or if there are some minor (or even major) tweaks you can make to produce better results.

Tips
- Keep a record of everything you do; write lists of how you spent your time, whom you contacted, etc.
- Create a proforma for any contacts you do make, with contact details, dates contacted, response and dates for follow-up.
- Always log your responses – whether it's an email, CV you've sent by mail or a phone call.
- Make notes about what went well, what went badly, what you could do better next time.
- Even if you don't get offers of work straight away, continue to keep records – people may contact you months (or even years!) later. If you don't keep records, how will you know you're not approaching the same people repeatedly?

It's really important to measure the effectiveness of the different forms of marketing against the cost. Whenever you pay for any form of marketing (from subscriptions to online services to membership fees of the SfEP or other organisations), record in a spreadsheet what it cost. Always try to find out how a client or enquiry came to you, so that you can record in the same spreadsheet how much income you have received through each channel. When it comes to renewing a subscription, you can see at a glance whether it was cost-effective and make a decision based on that. Of course, some things have other benefits – such as the social side of networking – so you need to bear that in mind as well. But if something is expensive and ineffective, you need to cut it out of your marketing plan.

Appendix

A basic checklist

1   Go back to basics – think about what you actually want to achieve and define your goals and objectives clearly. Make your goals easily achievable, setting yourself a target of writing a specific number (quite small) of letters or emails each week or month. That way you'll feel you've achieved something. These goals can be as small as 'Phone A today' or 'Email X, Y and Z by the end of the week'.
2   Do you want to get more business from current clients or work with new clients? Decide whom you're targeting (market sectors and specific clients) and make sure you target the right people in the right way to maximise results. The focus should be on gaining new clients, persuading current clients to use you more and getting inactive clients to return.
3   Decide what services you can offer your customers (existing and new) and be clear about what you're offering.
4   Sharpen up your image. How will you explain who you are and what you offer? Do you have a company name, logo, business cards, a website, a brochure, or at least a relevant CV? Get your marketing materials in shape, even if it's only a business card. You don't need to spend a fortune but do try to make them look professional. If you have a website, make sure it tells visitors what they need to know, and how to get in touch with you. Make sure that you update it regularly and that all links work.
5   Decide which methods you're going to use – some clients may need different approaches.
6   Get something down on paper – it doesn't matter how basic! It should be short, concise and easy to understand.

7   Little and often – don't wait until you're short of work to contact prospective clients. It's far better to market yourself little and often, even when you're overwhelmed with work. That way you should develop a steady stream of new business.

8   Keep your clients happy – stay in regular touch by phone or email to keep them up to date either with projects you're working on or with your future availability. Reassure them that you're doing everything that needs doing to deliver the project on time. Give your clients the opportunity to comment on work you've done; ask if they'd be happy to recommend you to someone else. You might like to try sending out a feedback form with your invoices, although you may find that people don't have the time to complete them. Ask for testimonials, which you can then use on your website or in your marketing literature. Respond quickly to enquiries from potential clients or from clients you're currently doing work for.

9   Make a plan and stick to it, but also accept that things will change and your plan will continue to evolve over the years.

10 Review progress regularly – look at what's working and what isn't, and refocus your efforts accordingly. Quantify results if possible. Learn from your past experiences – try to analyse which marketing tools were effective and which were unsuccessful, and ask yourself why, in order to refine and improve next year's marketing strategy.

Resources

Starting Out: Setting up a small business, 3rd edition, by Val Rice. SfEP, London

Editor and Client: Building a professional relationship, by Anne Waddingham. SfEP, London

SfEP website/wiki/SfEPLine/Associates Available

Editing Matters – the SfEP bi-monthly magazine contains lots of useful information on potential clients, as well as the occasional job advert

Writers' and Artists' Yearbook. Bloomsbury, London

Directory of British Associations [available to download from www.cbdresearch.com/DBA.htm]

Resumés for Freelancers by Sheila Buff. Editorial Freelancers Association, New York

Websites

Free directory websites

www.yell.com
www.touchlocal.com
www.thomsonlocal.com
www.hotfrog.co.uk
www.freeindex.co.uk
www.skillspages.com

Business advice

www.startups.co.uk
www.newbusiness.co.uk
www.smallbusiness.co.uk

Directory sites

Freelance Proofreaders: www.freelance-proofreaders.co.uk (currently £85/year)

Freelancers in the UK: www.freelancersintheuk.co.uk (currently £75/year).

The Professional Copywriters' Network: www.procopywriters.co.uk

Find a Proofreader: www.findaproofreader.com

PeoplePerHour: www.peopleperhour.com

Business support and networking organisations

National Union of Journalists: www.nuj.org.uk

British Chambers of Commerce: www.britishchambers.org.uk

Federation of Small Businesses: www.fsb.org.uk

Business Networking International (BNI): www.bni-europe.com

Business Referral Exchange: www.brxnet.co.uk

Publishing Training Centre: www.train4publishing.co.uk (if you've been on one of their distance learning courses you can be listed in their Freelance Finder database)

Society of Authors (www.societyofauthors.net)

Chartered Institute of Marketing (www.cim.co.uk)